In the Woods

Chris Wormell

Red Fox

Once there were three teddy bears who went for a walk in the woods.
Their names were Bubba, Rollo and Pog.

Bubba was the tallest, Rollo was the fattest (he was carrying the bag with their lunch) and Pog was the smallest and the most nervous. He didn't like woods.

They had not walked very far before Rollo said, "It must be time for a snack."
And he sat down on a tree stump and took an apple from the lunch bag.

Rollo was always hungry.

"We're not lost, are we?" asked Pog. "I think we're lost, I certainly don't

remember this part of the woods."

"No, we are not lost. I know the way," said Bubba. "And it's not time for a snack yet. Come on."

So off they went, further into the woods.

After a while Bubba, who was leading the way, stepped on a dry twig – crack!

"What was that?" yelped Pog. "Must be a wolf! I knew there'd be wolves. Help!"

"There are no wolves," assured Bubba. "It was only a twig."

Just then Rollo, who was the slowest, caught up with the other two.
   "It must be lunch time now. I'm so hungry!" he declared, peeling a banana.
   "No time for bananas. Come on," said Bubba.

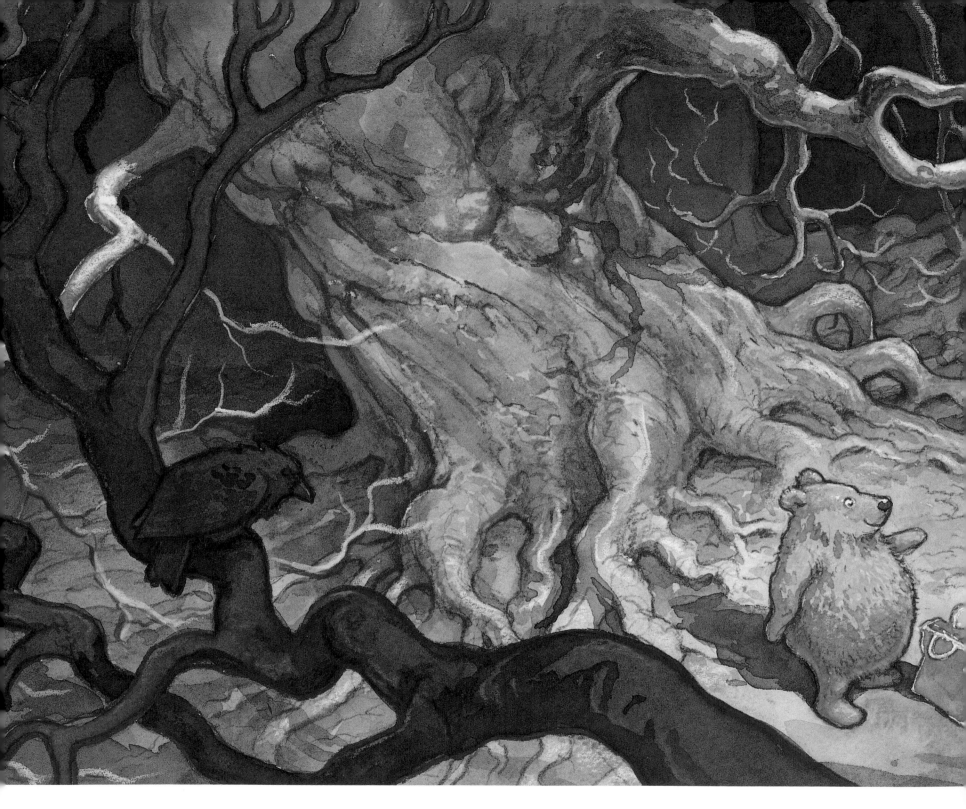

Soon they came to a place where the trees were crooked and twisted, with branches like claws.

"I don't like it here at all," moaned Pog. "And it's getting very dark. The big bad wolf is sure to come out at night."

When Rollo caught up he said, "What a perfect spot for a picnic!
We've got buns and cakes and all kinds of sandwiches and . . . "

"No time for that," snapped Bubba.

So off they went.

Further on, they came to a place where a fallen beech tree blocked the way.
Bubba frowned. "I don't remember this," he said.
"We *are* lost!" wailed Pog. "I knew we were lost!"

"Nonsense," said Bubba. "We'll be all right once we climb over. Give me your hand and I'll help you up. We'll have a rest and a little snack to keep us going."

"Snack?" exclaimed Rollo. "At last!"

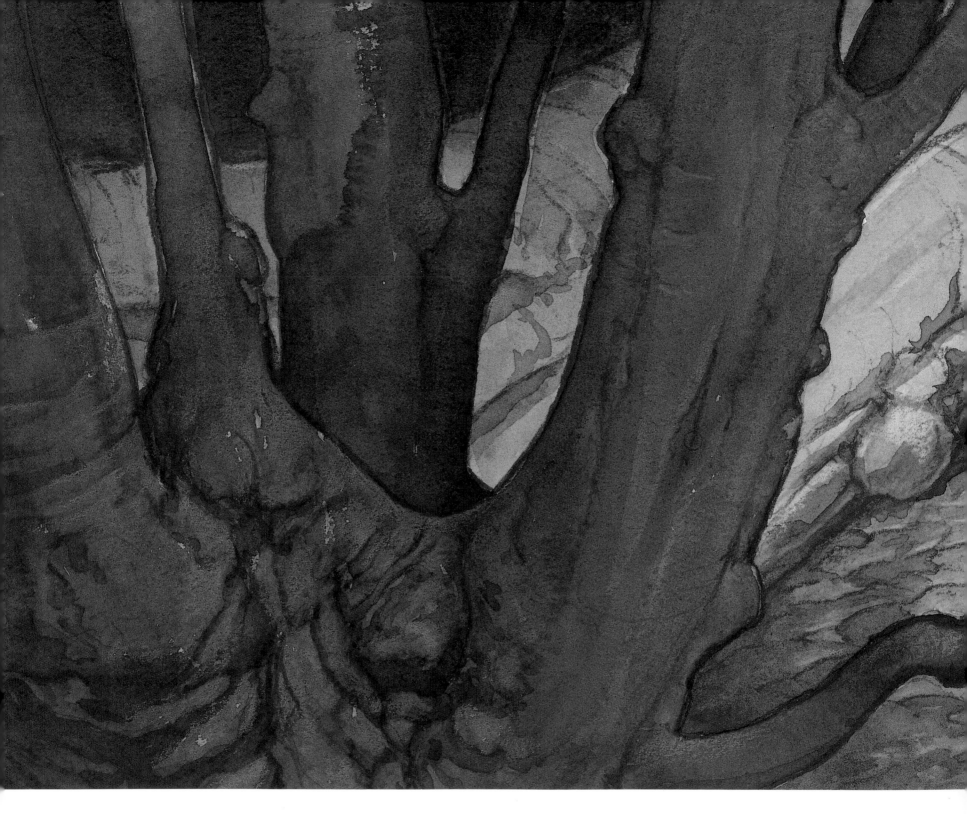

On the other side of the tree they all sat down and Rollo tipped up the lunch bag. Out rolled one small cake with pink icing and a cherry on top.

"Is that all there is?" asked Bubba. "Where's the rest of it? You haven't eaten it all, have you?"

"Oh, dear," said Rollo. "Er . . . these cakes are jolly nice. We could share it."

"Lost in the woods with no food!" wailed Pog. "We'll die of starvation – unless we're eaten by the wolf first!"

"Oh, do shut up about wolves, Pog," snapped Bubba. "There is NO wolf in this wood!"

But there was . . . and a little earlier, in another part of the wood, the wolf had found an apple core. He didn't like apples, but he could smell something else –

he could smell teddy bear. And the wolf did like teddy bear. His third favourite
dinner (after little pigs and little girls with red hoods) was teddy bear.

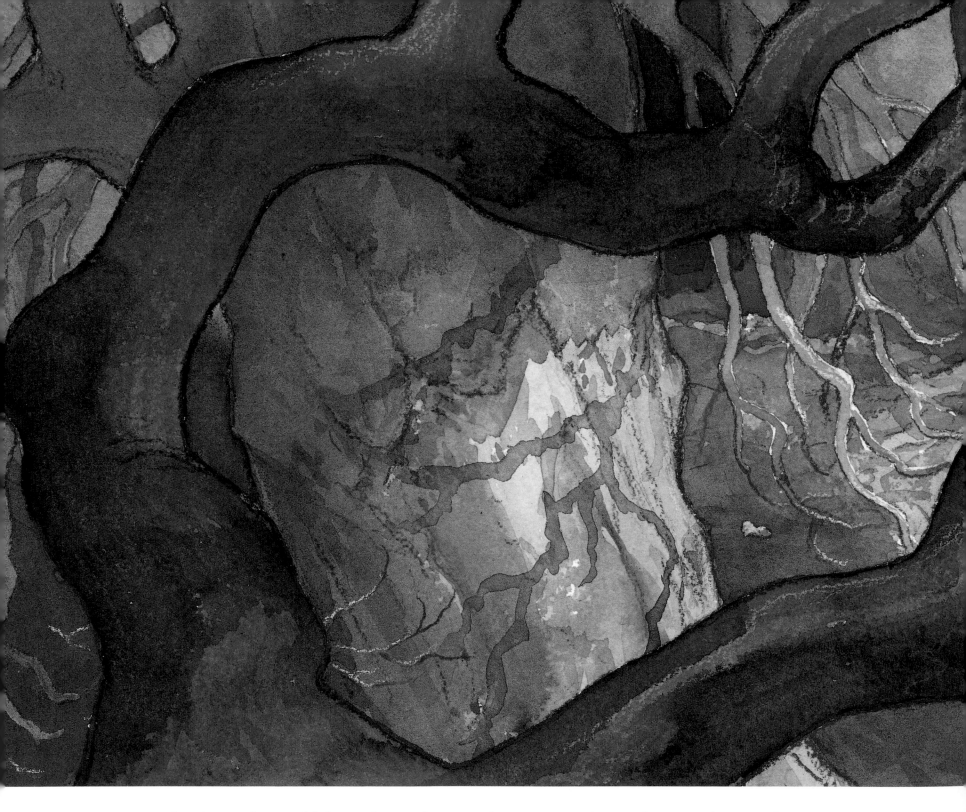

Further on, the wolf found another apple core, and another, and soon he was following a trail of banana skins and orange peel and sandwich corners.

The trail led right to the middle of the wood and all the while the smell of teddy bear grew stronger and stronger. The wolf began to lick his lips.

" . . . so do stop all this nonsense about wolves, Pog," went on Bubba. "And do close your mouth – there's nothing much to put in it, not now that greedy Rollo's eaten the picnic . . . What is the matter?"

Pog could only stutter, "Wo . . . wo . . . wo . . ."

"Help! There is a wolf," cried Bubba. "RUN!"

And they ran.

They ran as fast as they could. But not fast enough, and in no time at all poor Rollo could feel the wolf's hot breath on the back of his neck.

Then Bubba tripped on a root and fell and Pog and Rollo tumbled over him.
They all rolled and bumped and bounced and landed in a jumbled heap.

The wolf was standing right over them; his cruel yellow eyes staring and his enormous sharp teeth gleaming in his mouth.

Then suddenly a voice said, "Excuse me, Mr Wolf, but you are standing on my cucumber sandwich."

The wolf looked up and found himself surrounded by hundreds and
hundreds of other teddy bears: big ones, small ones, fat ones and thin ones
of very many different colours.

"This is a private picnic, Mr Wolf," said the bear with the squashed cucumber sandwich. "Teddy bears only!"

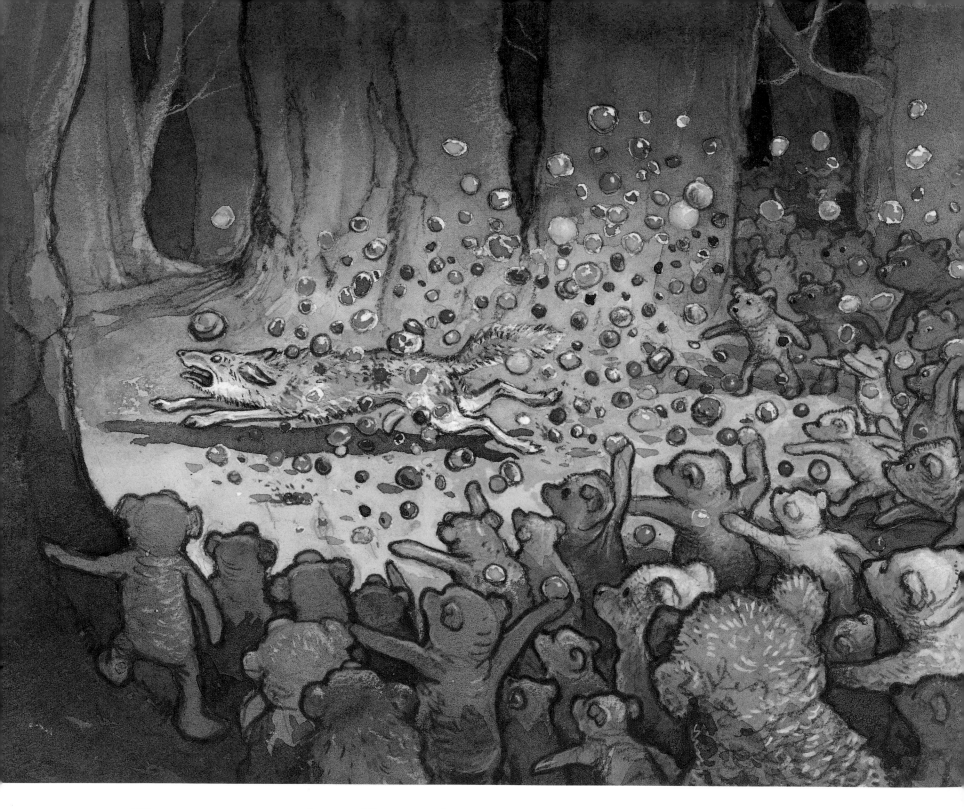

The next moment the wolf was pelted with apples and oranges and
melons and muffins and cakes and mangoes and squashy tomatoes
and nuts and hard-boiled eggs and bananas and empty honey pots

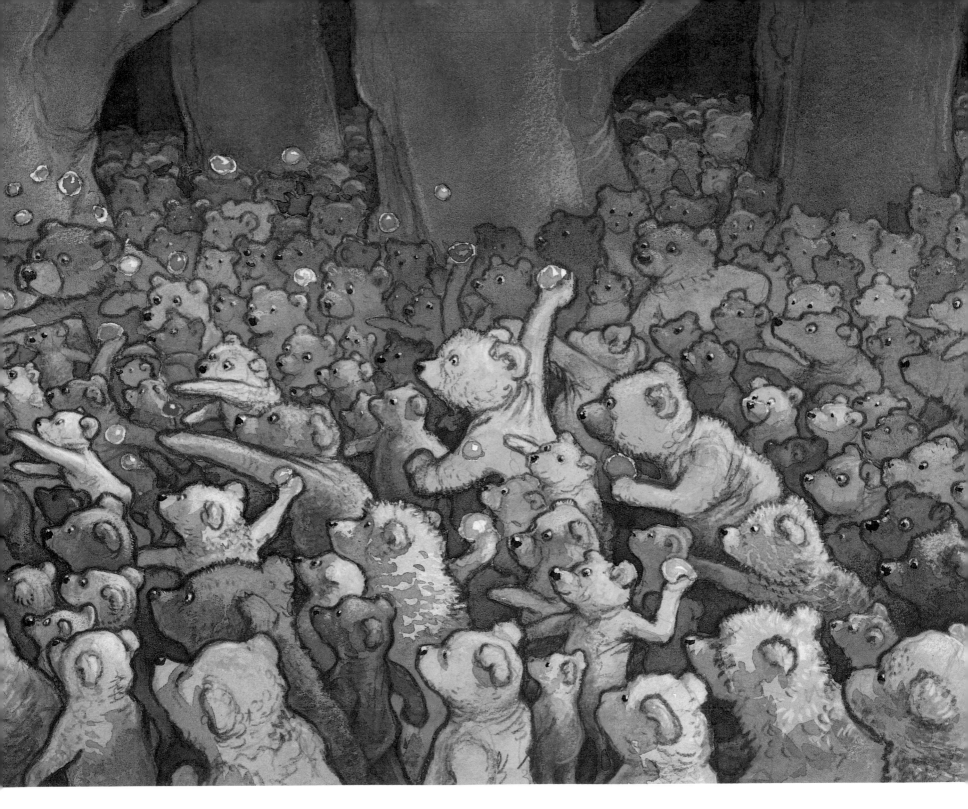

and a very stale, very hard pork pie which hit him right on the nose.
The wolf ran away as fast as he could.

A little while later, had you been in the woods that day, you might have heard a tremendous snoring noise, for nearly all the teddy bears were snoozing after eating as much food as they possibly could.

"I said I knew the way," mumbled Bubba in a sleepy voice, "and I was right."

"And I said there were wolves," said Pog with a yawn, "and I was right."

"And I said I was hungry," spluttered Rollo, stuffing an enormous slice of honey cake into his mouth, "and I was most certainly right!"

The wolf slunk away and hid in a thicket and didn't come out until the middle
of the night when all the bears had gone home to bed. He was very hungry by
then, but there was hardly a trace of the teddy bears' great picnic. Even the
stale pork pie had been eaten.

All that remained was one small cake with pink icing and a cherry on top.
And there was nothing the wolf hated more than pink icing.

For Eliza and Daisy

IN THE WOODS
A RED FOX BOOK 0 099 41767 7

First published in Great Britain by Jonathan Cape,
an imprint of Random House Children's Books

Jonathan Cape edition published 2003
Red Fox edition published 2004

3 5 7 9 10 8 6 4 2

Red Fox Books are published by Random House Children's Books,
61–63 Uxbridge Road, London W5 5SA,
a division of The Random House Group Ltd,
in Australia by Random House Australia (Pty) Ltd,
20 Alfred Street, Milsons Point, Sydney, NSW 2061, Australia,
in New Zealand by Random House New Zealand Ltd,
18 Poland Road, Glenfield, Auckland 10, New Zealand,
and in South Africa by Random House (Pty) Ltd,
Endulini, 5A Jubilee Road, Parktown 2193, South Africa

THE RANDOM HOUSE GROUP Limited Reg. No. 954009
www.kidsatrandomhouse.co.uk

A CIP catalogue record for this book is available from the British Library.

Printed in Singapore